For my mother, Sophia, who really did grow up by the sea and insisted I learn to swim. For my friend Sheila Barry, who encouraged me to share its secrets … sending my eternal love and thanks.

Deep Underwater

Irene Luxbacher

Groundwood Books
House of Anansi Press
Toronto Berkeley

Groundwood Books / House of Anansi Press
groundwoodbooks.com

We acknowledge for their financial support of our
publishing program the Canada Council for the Arts, the
Ontario Arts Council and the Government of Canada.

Canada Council   Conseil des Arts
for the Arts   du Canada

ONTARIO ARTS COUNCIL
CONSEIL DES ARTS DE L'ONTARIO
an Ontario government agency
un organisme du gouvernement de l'Ontario

With the participation of the Government of Canada
Avec la participation du gouvernement du Canada | Canada

FSC
www.fsc.org

MIX
Paper from
responsible sources
FSC® C012700

Library and Archives Canada Cataloguing in
Publication
Luxbacher, Irene, author, illustrator
Deep underwater / Irene Luxbacher.
Issued in print and electronic formats.
ISBN 978-1-77306-014-9 (hardcover).—
ISBN 978-1-77306-015-6 (PDF)
I. Title.
PS8623.U94D44 2018   jC813'.6   C2017-907485-7
C2017-907486-5

The art for this book was rendered by hand with
graphite, watercolor and acrylic paints, then digitally
composed and printed using archival inks and papers.
Final art was then further developed by hand with
graphite, soft-colored pencils and found
collage materials.
Design by Sara Loos and Michael Solomon
Printed and bound in Malaysia

My name is Sophia.
I live by the sea.

I know all its secrets.

I know where dragons live and
where floating forests grow.
I've seen clowns and angels and
four-eyed butterflies …

Will you dive down and see?
Will you follow me?

I know you will.
You are brave.

First, take a deep breath and
drift down, down past the day.
Stars can only shine when the
light fades.

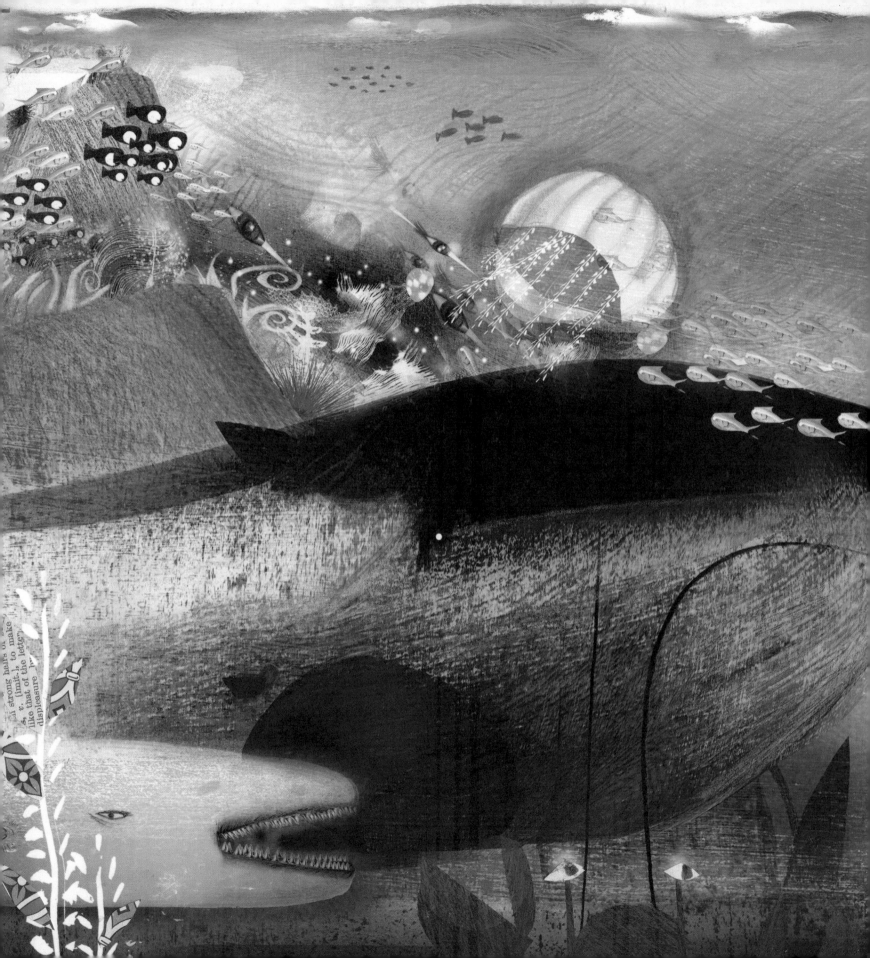

Deep underwater, tentacles,
antennae and teeth disappear into
darkness … and an abyss becomes
a bottomless pit of possibilities …

Here, hot gassy bubbles burp
ancient secrets from deep inside
the center of the Earth …

… and lost treasures
wait silently, patiently
hoping to be found.

Deep down, I never feel alone.

I can always see
a friend in me,
whose strength lifts me up …

like an ocean current …

and carries me home.